Grandpa & Jake

Julie Fortenberry

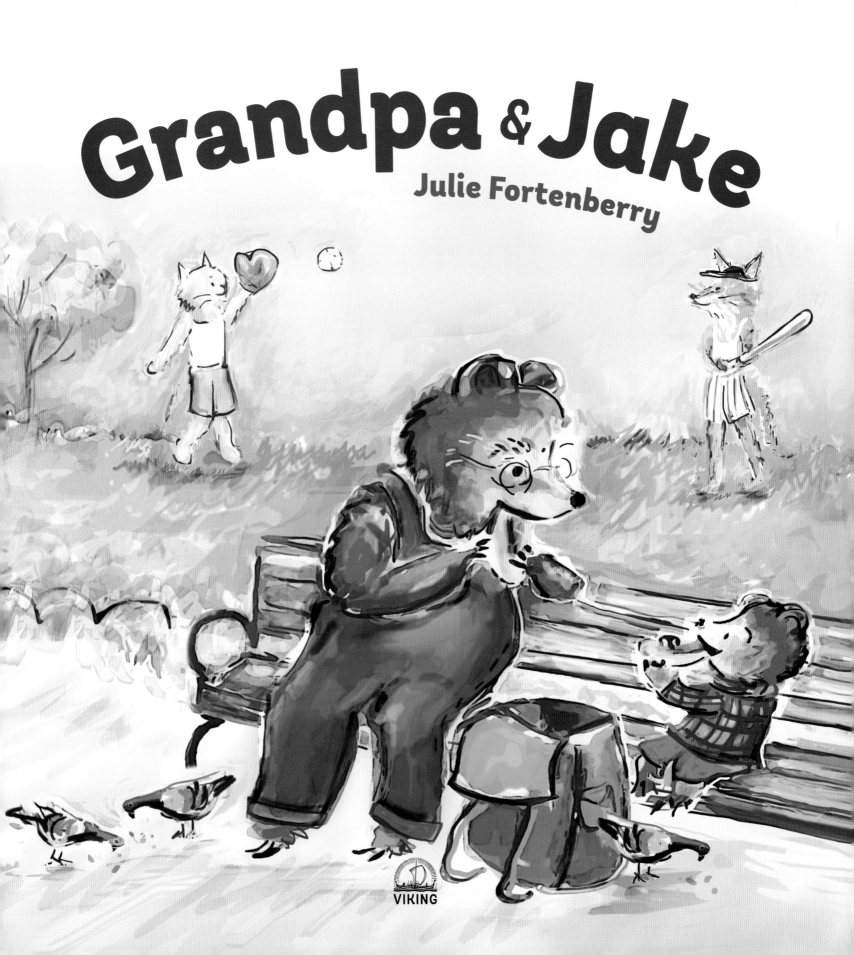

VIKING

"Let's turn the TV off," said Jake's grandpa.
"But I love this show!" said Jake. "It's not over yet."

"Here, let's get your jacket on.
There's someplace I'd like to show you.
A place my grandpa took *me* when I was your age."
  "Where is it?" asked Jake.
  "You have to guess. I think you'll like it."
  "Why? Are there dinosaurs there?" asked Jake.
  "Maybe," said Grandpa.

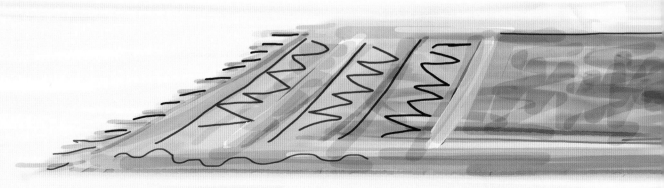

"Are we going to pick peaches? I love peaches!"
"I think we'll do that later," said Grandpa.

"Are we going on a boat?" asked Jake. "I love boats!"
"No, but when we get there we can see *all kinds* of boats."

"Did your grandpa take you fishing?"
"No, he never did."

"Are we going to the beach?
I love the beach!"
"No," said Grandpa. "It's inside."

"Grandpa? Are you sure
you know where you're going?"
"Yep. It's inside with boats."

"Inside with boats? And pirates?
We must be going to the movies!
I love the movies!"
"Well, no," said Grandpa.

"So no popcorn? But I love popcorn. And I'm *hungry . . .*"

"I know," said Grandpa.
"But look—we can eat hot dogs
right here."

"Grandpa, did your grandpa ever take you to a ball game?"
"He did, but we're not doing that today."

"Okay, Jake . . . just up these steps.
Now take my hand and close your eyes."

"It's not safe to walk around
with your eyes closed, Grandpa."
"Just for a second, Jake."

"Now open your eyes," whispered Grandpa.

**"WOW! I LOVE IT HERE!
I'VE ALWAYS WANTED TO COME
HERE! WHERE ARE WE?"**

"*Shhhh.*
It's a library, Jake."

"**WOW! LOOK AT ALL THE BOOKS! I LOVE BOOKS!**

Oops! Sorry, Grandpa.

Look at all the books! I love books!"

There are books
about baseball . . .

books about
boats . . .

books about
pirates . . .

books about
dinosaurs . . .

books about
peaches . . .

and books about books!

"You must have loved your grandpa," whispered Jake.
"I did. And he loved me too," whispered Grandpa.

"Okay, Jake. Time to go. The library is closing."
"But we just got here! I haven't finished my book yet!"

"I NEVER WANT TO LEAVE!

I'm not going!

I'm not going!

I'm not going!"

"Well, if you don't go now, you won't get to check that book out," said Grandpa.

"WHAT DOES *THAT* MEAN?"

"*Shhh* . . . you can borrow it. It means you can take it home. And you can borrow a few more books. Just as long as you return them."

"Wow," said Jake, "I love this!"

"Grandpa? Are we going home now?"
"Yep."
"Will you read to me when
we get home?"
"I'd love to."

For John Thurman

VIKING

An imprint of Penguin Random House LLC, New York

First published in the United States of America by Viking, an imprint of Penguin Random House LLC, 2022

Visit us online at penguinrandomhouse.com.

Library of Congress Cataloging-in-Publication Data is available.

Manufactured in China

ISBN 9780593404355

Special Markets ISBN 9780593623312 Not for resale

3   5   7   9   10   8   6   4   2

RRD

Design by Jim Hoover   Text set in Andes

This Imagination Library edition is published by Penguin Young Readers, a division of Penguin Random House LLC, exclusively for Dolly Parton's Imagination Library, a not-for-profit program designed to inspire a love of reading and learning, sponsored in part by The Dollywood Foundation. Penguin's trade editions of this work are available wherever books are sold.